John Edward Raisbeck

The Lion and the Eagle

A Comedy in Three Acts

John Edward Raisbeck

The Lion and the Eagle
A Comedy in Three Acts

ISBN/EAN: 9783744783170

Printed in Europe, USA, Canada, Australia, Japan

Cover: Foto ©Andreas Hilbeck / pixelio.de

More available books at **www.hansebooks.com**

THE

LION AND THE EAGLE

A Comedy in Three Acts.

By JOHN E. RAISBECK.

CINCINNATI:

GEO. E. BRYAN, THEATRICAL PRINTER AND ENGRAVER,
58 West Fourth Street.

CHARACTERS.

JOHN BLASSY, a British bottle manufacturer, visiting the United States in the interests of his business. He is a fat Yorkshireman.

SIR CHARLES WORMLEY, a young British peer, taking his second pleasure trip to America.

TOM BLASSY, a son of John Blassy, and a friend of Sir Charles Wormley, visiting America for the first time.

ROBERT ROSEWELL, a rich American returning from a European trip with his two daughters and a widowed sister.

GEORGE DUCKERSON, a New York museum manager, and uncle to the girls; also returning from Europe with his wife.

JAKE, a negro musician.

GEORGIE ROSEWELL, a sharp, lively, caustic, and patriotic American girl. Daughter to Robert Rosewell.

CLARA ROSEWELL, her sister; more subdued, refined, and ladylike.

MRS. ALICE HARPLEY, a widow, and sister of Mr. Rosewell.

MRS. NELLIE DUCKERSON, wife of George Duckerson, and sister of Mr. Rosewell and Mrs. Harpley.

KATE, a mulatto girl at Mr. Rosewell's.

Bowery boys, sailors, officers, etc.

SCENERY.

ACT I, ... On Board the Servia.
Scene—Outside Sandy Hook.

ACT II, ... Washington and New York.
Scene 1—Parlor in Mr. Rosewell's house, Washington.
Scene 2—The Bowery, New York City.
Scene 3—Duckerson's office in his New York theater.

ACT III, ... At Mr. Rosewell's.
Scene 1—Conservatory and grounds around the house.
Scene 2—The kitchen.

TIME—The Present.

COSTUMES.

ACT I.

First part of Scene—Georgie and Clara in careless, every-day clothes, such as are usually worn by people on shipboard.

Latter part of Scene—All in the latest styles of traveling costumes.

ACT II.

Scene 1—Georgie and Clara in morning wrappers. Kate in shabby dress, handkerchief on head, shoes unbuttoned. Mr. Rosewell in morning gown, slippers, smoking cap, etc. Mrs Harpley in walking dress, hat, etc., suitable for shopping.

Scene 2—Blassy in business suit slightly disordered, hard round felt hat on one side. Bowery boys in all sorts of old clothes. Sir Charles in dark frock coat and vest, light trousers, high light hat, blonde wig parted in center, blonde side whiskers and mustache, cane, gloves, etc. Tom Blassy in fashionable sack coat, gray trousers, light low-crowned hat, black mustache, no whiskers, cane, gloves, etc. George Duckerson in light summer suit, sack coat, light high hat, black mustache. Mrs. Duckerson in dress of some light stuff, parasol, etc.

Scene 3—Georgie in handsome, stylish walking dress, parasol, gloves, hat, etc. Clara in suit somewhat different from Georgie's, but equally elegant.

ACT III.

All in full evening dress, but John Blassy's is old-fashioned.

THE LION AND THE EAGLE.

ACT I.

SCENE.—*A steamer just outside of Sandy Hook, approaching New York. Officer on the bridge, peering through his glass at the sea in the distance. As the curtain rises, four or five sailors (good singers) are discovered working the chain and singing the following song:*

> What joy there is on a gallant bark,
>   Controlled by a gallant band,
> None but a fearless sailor lad
>   Can ever understand.
> The wild delights of a sailor's life
>   'Tis useless to explain
> To those who've never seen the seas,
>   And crossed the Spanish Main.
>
> *Chorus.*—Don't speak of pleasures of home life
>   To men so bold and free.
>   A sailor's life is a jovial life;
>   A sailor's life for me!
>
> We go to islands of the seas,
>   Where white men seldom go;
> And pluck the fruit from tropic trees,
>   Or brush the Alpine snow.
> What'er we do, where'er we go,
>   We sailors still remain—
> We sing and smoke and take our ease,
>   And dream of Betsey Jane.
>
> *Chorus.*—Don't speak of pleasures of home life
>   To men so bold and free.
>   A sailor's life is a jovial life;
>   A sailor's life for me!

As they finish singing the last line a ringing laugh by Georgie is heard on the outside, and immediately enter Georgie and Clara, rather carelessly dressed.

CLARA. There! there! Georgie! Don't be so rude. I am positively ashamed of you. You are much too—— ,.

GEORGIE. How *can* I help being amused at that—that— (what do they call it in the newspapers?) —that noble scion of an effete monarchy? With his eye-glass stuck in his eye half the time like an idiot.

CLARA. What language! Really I should not like Sir Charles to hear you. He would say you——

GEORGIE. I don't care what he would say. It is the last day on board, and I shall say what I please I intend to give him a piece of my mind, if I get a chance, for the many sneers he has cast at my country. Besides, what is he to me? I never expect to see him again.

CLARA. That is no reason why you should speak disrespectfully of him. I much fear, however, that away down in that little heart of yours you *do* expect to see him again.

GEORGIE. No, I don't. (*Slight pause.*) Or if I do, he will have to change his tone about America and everything American. My own self-respect——

CLARA. (*Archly.*) He *will* change his tone about *one* thing American.

GEORGIE. Don't be foolish. You see further with your eyes than your judgment.

CLARA. Time will tell. But, after all, we have had a delightful time on board. Now, haven't we?

GEORGIE. Oh, yes. Although I think (mind, I only *think*) that if it had not been for Mr. Blassy, the younger (*your* very particular friend), and that popinjay, Sir Charles, our voyage would have been rather monotonous.

CLARA. (*Laughing slightly.*) Look out, now. Be careful what you say.

GEORGIE. But he *is* a popinjay

CLARA. Then you have fallen in love with a popinjay, and I am sure you would marry him were he to ask you.

GEORGIE. (*Stamping her foot.*) Never!

CLARA. Yes, you would. Just think of what——

GEORGIE. I say never! never!

CLARA. Just think of what he is heir to—paternal grounds, baronial halls, ancestral trees, and—and a title.

GEORGIE. (*Mimicking.*) And—and a title. I guess *you*

would like the title. (*Sarcastically.*) You should set your cap for him, my dear—or your bangs.

CLARA. No; I would not set my cap for his title, nor (*smoothing her hair*)—nor my bangs either. But I might for his ancestral estates. So beware of me, Georgie. You know I love anything that has age to it; and the ancestral estates of England have the aroma of a thousand years. We may transplant and imitate, but we can not give to our buildings the ancestral aroma.

GEORGIE. Why, Clara, you are quite an **Anglomaniac**. Before long you will be despising your own country—*you*, the sensible Clara. *I* am an American.

CLARA. And so am I. But that does not prevent me from admiring things in other countries unknown in ours, just the same as foreigners admire things in our country unknown in theirs. And Sir Charles Wormley has had the justice to admit that it is possible to live in America.

GEORGIE. *Possible*, indeed! *Possible* to live in America! And you think I would marry a man who talks in that supercilious style about *my* country—a prating fool, who talks as though he had a pebble in his mouth—a dolt, who wears a single eye glass. Never!

CLARA. What dreadful language! I wish you would be a little more choice in the use of words. Georgie.

GEORGIE. It is only a habit of mine.

CLARA. And it is only a habit that Sir Charles has of wearing an eye-glass. He certainly does not *talk* like a fool, as you call him; for even *you* have been forced to admit the justness of some of his remarks about America, and——

GEORGIE. No, I have admitted nothing. I am always and ever an American; and no Sir Charles Wormley can make me be anything else—unless I wish to.

CLARA. When, for instance, he said that politics in America at election times always reminded him of the witches' cauldron in "Macbeth," the only difference being that the cauldron of politics was continually boiling over and somebody getting smirched. And when you replied that that was because we liked our stew hot, did you not admit——

GEORGIE. (*With a ringing laugh.*) Why, I admitted nothing. Didn't you see by my answer that I did not think his criticism worth a gooseberry?

CLARA. Perhaps not. However, I think Sir Charles is quite sensible.

GEORGIE. I suppose you do. It is a wonder you do not

marry him. For my part, I think him insufferably insolent, supercilious, egotistical, vainglorious, bigoted——

CLARA. Stop! stop! Georgie! Perhaps you are equally so to him.

GEORGIE. (*Laughing loudly at the thought.*) I hope so; I hope so. Indeed, I do.

A voice is heard outside.

CLARA. Be quiet. They are coming.

GEORGIE. I won't. I'll laugh the more.

> *Georgie laughs again, Clara grasps her arm, and they retire up R., and look out upon the sea. Enter at the same time Sir Charles Wormley and Tom Blassy, L., both dressed for traveling. Sir Charles holds his eye-glass in his left hand, looks rather namby-pambyish, but is withal shrewd and sarcastic. Tom is a manly looking young fellow, and dressed to contrast somewhat.*

SIR C. (*Drawlingly.*) There she goes again—fairly howling with vacant and idiotic laughter. There is nothing that so soon gives me a mental nausea as vacant laughter.

TOM. Do you call that vacant laughter?

SIR C. Yes What do you call it?

TOM. I call it a merry, girlish laugh.

SIR C. Tut, tut! There is nothing girlish about it, and nothing very merry. It is affectation, my boy—affectation— too forced to be natural.

TOM. But very winsome, withal.

SIR C. Only to a fledgling.

TOM. Like myself, for instance.

SIR C. Exactly.

TOM. I envy your effrontery

SIR C. I know you do, and would imitate it if you could. But I was about to say, Tom—remember we are on shipboard, and not in America yet, else I would not dare to say it.

TOM. Well, go on.

SIR C. (*Looking around, and motioning with his finger in the direction of Georgie and Clara.*) No American ladies can hear us, can they?

TOM. I should scarcely think so.

GEORGIE. (*Aside to Clara.*) I wonder what they are talking about.

CLARA. Oh, about billiards and cigars, I suppose—what young men usually talk about.

They unconsciously draw nearer, and overhear the following:

SIR C. Well, I was about to say that forced laughter is a peculiarity of the American ladies—perhaps I should call it a national failing; for all the ladies laugh unnecessarily, especially when entertaining company, and all the girls giggle immoderately at the most commonplace remarks.

CLARA. (*To Georgie, who has clenched her hands and become terribly excited.*) Oh, why—why did we listen to this? Come away, Georgie. Come.   [*Georgie is immovable.*]

TOM. A result, perhaps, of their naturally high spirits.

SIR C That is exactly the impwession they wish to convey. But by watching them closely you perceive that it is mostly, as I said before, affectation—thrown in partly to fill up the pauses in conversation, and partly to be thought lively and entertaining. A sham, my deah boy; and I detest shams.

> *Georgie gnashes her teeth, and Clara with difficulty prevents her from rushing at Sir Charles.*

TOM. I fear you are prejudiced. Perhaps you have been jilted by some fair American, who was too independent to sell herself for your title

SIR C. No, no. 'Pon my honah, no.

TOM. If not that, then there must be something else. But I think you said that the women as well as the girls——

SIR C. (*Putting his hand on Tom's arm.*) Stop where you are, Tom; you have misunderstood me. I did not say the *women;* I said the *ladies.*

TOM. The what?

SIR C. The ladies.

TOM. But—I—I do not understand you. Tell me what you are talking about. Are not women ladies?

SIR C. Yes; but ladies are not women—in America.

TOM. (*Pausing and arching his eyebrows.*) I fail to penetrate.

SIR C. No doubt; and there will be many things, my deah fellow, you will fail to penetwate before you get through.

TOM. What a peculiar people the Americans must be.

SIR C. Yes, a vewy peculiar people.

> *Georgie makes another effort to get at Sir Charles, but is prevented by Clara.*

SIR C. (*Continuing.*) Even the washerwomen and the servants (female *help*, I should say) would be insulted did you call them women. (*Slapping him on the shoulder.*) They are all ladies, my deah boy—all ladies.

TOM. What about the negresses that I shall see?

SIR C. Well, they are not negresses now.

TOM. No? Good Lord, what are they?

Sir C.   They are—*colored* ladies.

Tom.   (*At a loss for words to express his thoughts suitably.*) You
stagger me!   I am bewildered!   I—I fail to pene rate.

Sir C.   Watch your speech, Tom; watch your speech—if
you do not want to be thought rude   You must not, for instance, speak of the barnyard fowls as anything but roosters
and chickens.   They have no cocks and hens.   They do not
know what they are.   You must be vewy particular about this

Tom.   *Very* particular about it?

Sir C.   Vewy.

Tom.   But I say, Charles, have they no dictionaries?

Sir C.   Lots of dictionaries, but few weaders.   Every man
is a dictionary unto himself, especially the editors.

Tom.   No, no, no, Charles; you can not make me believe
everything.   When you attempt to cast a slur at ye gentle
editor, I shall have to draw the line.   Besides, he will cut your
head off—with his pen—if he hears you.

Sir C.   No fear.   There's none on board.

Tom.   But what makes you say the editors are dictionaries
unto themselves?

Sir C.   Why, because they are continually twying to reform
the language or to coin new words.   One first-class paper, for
instance, spells philosophy, philanthropy, and such like words
with an *f;* and another will have nothing to do with the word
"manufacturer," but always pwints it "facturer."

Tom.   What a strange people!   Every editor a dictionary.
And what a singular way to study brevity.   If "brevity is the
soul of wit," then their papers must be very witty.   I shall like
to read their papers.   Full of strange thoughts, no doubt.

Sir C.   (*Sarcastically.*) Brimful, brimful.   And one thing
more, my deah fellow, I must caution you about.   Nevah speak
of *shops* to a lady; it is too suggestive of machine shops, or
something of that sort.   You must call them *stores.*

Tom.   Call shops stores?

Sir C.   Yes.

Tom.   Then, of course, it will not do for me to ask a lady if
she has been *shopping;* for if the English go shopping in shops,
it necessarily follows that the Americans go storing in stores.
I must therefore ask her if she has been *storing.*

Sir C.   By no means.

Tom.   No?   What a peculiar people!

Sir C.   A *vewy* peculiar people.

Georgie.   (*Stepping up, no longer able to control herself.*) Mr.
Blassy, allow me to inform you that we do not go storing in

stores. We go *shopping* in stores. When we have any *storing* to do, we do it by storing our goods *in* the store. Now, do you understand? (*Turning to Sir Charles defiantly.*) And if Sir Charles Wormley has anything more——

CLARA. (*More subdued.*) I think, Mr. Blassy, that Sir——

GEORGIE. *Will* you let me speak, Clara?

CLARA. Not just now, dear; you are too excited. Mr. Blassy, I think Sir Charles is imposing a little upon your credulity. You will find that we are not such a *very* peculiar people as he would have you believe. We have our peculiarities, it is true; but——

SIR C. I was not aware that our conversation had the honah of being listened to by—*ladies.*

Turns and takes a few steps up L. *with Tom.*

GEORGIE. (*Angrily.*) I suppose you think, *Sir Charles*, that we ought to stand quietly by, *Sir Charles*, and hear insults, *Sir Charles*—yes, sir, insults—heaped upon us by a picayunish English lord!

CLARA. Oh, Georgie! Georgie!

SIR C. (*Aside to Tom*) I say, my deah boy, you like spunk There is spunk for you.

TOM. Too much spunk *for you*, I should say.

SIR C. (*Coolly adjusting his eye-glass.*) Ladies, will you permit me to remark——

GEORGIE. We don't want to hear any remarks from a man who wears a glass in his eye, parts his hair in the middle, puts on puppy airs, talks as if he had a hot potato in his mouth, and looks like a Chimpanzee.

CLARA. Georgie, dear, please don't talk so. It is shameful. Let us all part friends. Remember this is our last day on board.

GEORGIE. I am going to speak my mind first. And while I am about it, Sir Charles, since you have been so free in expressing yourself about the Americans, let me tell you what I think about the English I think they are the most arrogant, the most selfish, and the most egotistical people on the face of the earth; and that Sir Charles Wormley is the most arrogant (*Clara takes hold of Georgie's arm, and shakes it in an effort to stop her*), the most selfish, and the most egotistical of them all! There!

Clara throws up her arms in despair, and Georgie walks excitedly across the stage.

SIR C. (*Aside to Tom.*) Gweat country for divo'ces, is America.

TOM. (*Significantly.*) I should almost think so.

Enter Mr. John Blassy and Mr. Rosewell, R. *Mr. Blassy
is a very fat man, of true Falstaffian proportions, about
fifty years of age, and wearing very big English walking
shoes. Mr. Rosewell is about the same age, but rather
slender and genteel looking. Blassy has a Yorkshire
accent, but not too broad. Both are dressed for landing.*

BLASSY. What! What! Tom, me lad, quarreling with the
lasses? Nay, this will never do. When I was thy age, I—
(*turning and observing Georgie's flushed face*). And you, Miss
Georgie. quarreling with *my* son? (*Tapping her under the
chin.*) Come, come, me lass; a pout does not become this
dimpled chin.

GEORGIE. No, Mr Blassy, I am *not* quarreling with your
son; I am quarreling with his friend there—that insolent sprig
of nobility.

BLASSY. What, Sir Charles? Nay, I can not believe that.
I always thought Sir Charles too much of a gentleman.

SIR C. I assure you, Mr. Blassy, that I nevah quaweled
with a lady in my life, and I do not intend that the charming
Miss Rosewell shall be the first.

BLASSY. I thought so, I thought so. So mak' it up, me
lass. Shake hands. Life is too short to waste it foolishly, as
a greater man than me has said. (*Looks at his stomach.*)

MR. R. Yes, my dears, you may as well be friendly with
these young gentlemen. I have invited Mr. Blassy to pay us a
visit in the fall; and he will, of course, bring his son and Sir
Charles with him.

CLARA. How very good of you, papa. I'm sure we will do
our best to entertain them.

GEORGIE. (*Aside to Clara.*) Never! If *he* comes, I go.

MR. R. Quite right, Clara; and I hope Georgie will show
the same obliging spirit.

BLASSY. For, of course, Mr. Rosewell, if the young uns are
not pleasant together, it would mak' it very *on*pleasant for me.
So now, Tom, brace up, and be a good lad.

TOM. Why, father, I have none but the kindliest feelings
for the ladies.

CLARA. (*Moving toward Sir Charles.*) And I, for my part,
have nothing against the young gentlemen.

*Clara takes Sir Charles' arm, seeing which Georgie takes
Tom's.*

CLARA. (*Aside.*) Perhaps this will excite her jealousy a
little. We women are queer creatures.

GEORGIE. (*Aside.*) She thinks I don't see through her little scheme. But I do. I know she prefers Mr. Blassy.

[*Exeunt, one couple* L., *the other* R.

BLASSY. Now, as I was saying when we tumbled on them youngs uns a fighting, facts is facts, business is business, and friendship is friendship.

MR. R. All very true, Mr. Blassy—all very true.

BLASSY. Which being the case, you will exert yourself, for friendship's sake, to repeal the duty on glass. For me it will be business, and your reward will be a fact. (*Slaps him on the shoulder.*) I may say, Mr. Rosewell, a *varry substantial* fact.

MR. R. You could not, perhaps, be more definite, and explain how substantial *the fact* will be.

BLASSY. Well, no, not just now; but four ciphers will partly express it. Of course, you will exert yourself personally, Mr. Rosewell—do, in fact, a little lobbying. I believe that's what you call it.

MR. R. Yes, that is our polite term for boring and buttonholing our Congressmen. You may depend upon me to do my utmost to further your interests, Mr. Blassy. And, furthermore, I will engage Mrs. Harpley, my sister, to help us. The ladies, sir, are the most successful lobbyists in our country.

BLASSY. (*With a surprised look.*) Indeed! Well! well! well! But, then, what can't woman do? Nay, is there anything on this hemispherical globe that woman can not do? Poor, puny man must seek her aid in everything. Woman! woman!

MR. R. Why, Mr. Blassy, you are quite tragic.

BLASSY. (*With a feeble smile.*) Yes, I was a poet once.

MR. R. Ha! ha! ha! Impossible! Once a poet, always a poet. Poets, you know, are born, not made.

BLASSY. Fact, I assure you. There was once a time when this portly form was as light as the downy web of a fairy's wing.

MR. R. Why, you are quite poetical still. (*Shyly scanning his person.*) But that must have been in the long, long ago.

BLASSY. Not so long as a dull sermon, nor so short as a lover's walk; but it was before Age had plucked me by the beard, and Time had not reared this monument of flesh to curse my later days. (*Putting his hands on his stomach.*)

MR. R. Mr. Blassy, I would advise you to cultivate the muses by all means—if you can reduce your flesh. They do not go well together, and—— (*Merry voices are heard on the outside.*) Here comes that perennial bore, my brother-in-law. You must excuse him if he sometimes——

*Enter George Duckerson, with **Mrs.** Duckerson and Mrs.
Harpley on his arms. Duckerson is a lively, hail-fellow-
well-met sort of man, **and the ladies are also** jolly. They
are about thirty-five **years of age, and are** dressed for
traveling*

DUCKERSON. Here, you old graybeards, are you never——
MRS. HARPLEY. Mr. Blassy, I shall have to take you under
my wing once more if you don't——
MRS. DUCKERSON. Robert, are you going to keep Mr.
Blassy here talking until the last minute?
MR. R. My dear sisters, we are all ready. Only our trunks
to look after.
MRS. H. And that, you know, is the most important thing.
Is it not, Mr. Blassy?
BLASSY. If the ladies say so, Mrs. Harpley, it must be so.
MRS. D. (*Aside to her husband.*) Charming old man. Alice
is just—*you* know.
DUCK. (*Ready to burst with laughter*) Well, I should say I
do know.
MR. R. I will go below and see what the girls are doing.
Now, Mr. Blassy, don't forget to visit us, and we will endeavor
to make your stay as pleasant as possible.
Exit Mr. Rosewell, the ladies accompanying him to the door.
MRS. H. (*Speaking after him.*) Robert, tell Clara to look
after my sachel.
MRS. D. (*Also speaking after him.*) And tell Georgie not to
talk to that young officer too much, or I shall tell Sir Chawles.
They both laugh heartily, retire up C., *and gaze upon the sea.*
DUCK. (*To Mr. Blassy.*) I say, old man, I guess you have
yet some smack of youth in you, eh?—some relish for the salt-
ness of the flesh?
BLASSY. I don't exactly——
DUCK. No, you don't exactly catch on—no, of course not.
BLASSY. (*Looking bewildered.*) As Tom says, I fail to pene-
trate.
DUCK. Why now, look here, I know a sweet creature that's
just gone on you.
BLASSY. (*With a loud guffaw.*) Ha! ha! ha! I never
thought you could be so interesting. Tell me more about it.
DUCK. And I'll bet you five dollars you don't know who
it is.
BLASSY. It cartainly can't be Mrs. Ducker——
DUCK. Look out, old man.

BLASSY. Well, I give it up.

DUCK. That's good enough. **If you don't know who it is,** then I've done talking about it. **You certainly are an old stick.** I dare **say,** though, **you** have known the time that you could have crept through a bride's wedding ring. (*Smiles and looks at Blassy from head to foot.*)

BLASSY. I've heerd say as the Americans is a 'umorous people. I suppose *you* are a 'umorous American.

DUCK. Yes, a little that way. But now for a few words on business, John.

BLASSY. (*With dignity.*) *Mr. Blassy,* if you please.

DUCK. All right. Blassy then it is.

Blassy looks at him with withering scorn, but says nothing

DUCK. (*Continuing*) It's a delicate subject; but I've made up my mind to ask you, this being the last day we shall be together I've been over to Europe seeking artists and curiosities. Now, how would you like me to engage you as a curiosity for my museum?

BLASSY. (*Disgustedly.*) Sir?

DUCK. You would have nothing to do but sit on a platform in two chairs instead of one, and smile at the ladies all day.

BLASSY. (*More disgustedly.*) 'Pon my soul, sir, I never——

DUCK. I know you never exhibited. But that is nothing. Don't let that worry you. (*Slaps him good-humoredly*) Think it over, Mr. Blassy—think it over. Your fortune is made.

[*Exit Mr. Duckerson.*

BLASSY. (*In a rage.*) And is it come to this that I, a representative British merchant, a man with wealth enough to buy all the beggarly museums in the country—that *I* should be insulted at every turn, upon a British ship, by an enterprising Yankee showman? Now, by all me forefathers, I want an apology—I want satisfaction—I want revenge. (*Struts around.*)

The ladies turn around suddenly, run, and each catch an arm.

MRS. H. Why, Mr. Blassy, what is the matter?

MRS. D. I never saw you in such a passion before. You must have encountered something fearful.

MRS. H. Or been abused terribly.

BLASSY. (*Calming down.*) I *have* been abused, ladies. Me feelings have been hurt—I may say stabbed. I have (I am ashamed to say it)—I have been asked to join a museum as a curiosity.

MRS. D. Oh, I am sure George did not mean to insult you, Mr. Blassy. It is merely a matter of business with him.

Mrs. H. That is all, Mr. Blassy. And where no offense is intended, you know, none should be taken.

Blassy. (*Patting them under the chin.*) Well spoken, me dears. Perhaps it is as you say.

Mrs. D. (*Aside to Mrs. H*) It may have been one of George's dreadful jokes.

Mrs. H. Just possible.

Mrs. D. But upon what grounds did he wish to engage you, Mr. Blassy?

Mrs II. Yes, why did he wish to exhibit you as a curiosity?

Mrs. D. You are not deformed in any way.

Mrs. H. Nor yet capable of writing with your foot and that sort of thing.

Blassy. (*Looking doubtfully at them.*) Well, now, if *you* don't know, I'm sure *I* don't know. Perhaps it was me superb good nature he wanted to exhibit.

Mrs. D. Ha! ha! ha! Do you believe that a good-natured man is so great a curiosity?

Blassy. Me fifty years of life have led me to believe so

Mrs. H. I think, Mr. Blassy, you are about right. Thoroughly good-natured men are as scarce as fifty-dollar bills in a tenement house.

> *Enter Sir Charles and Clara,* L., *and Tom and Georgie* R. *The girls have changed their dresses, and are now ready for landing.*

Clara. Come, aunties—both of you—the steward says we shall be landing in two hours, and that we had all better be getting ready. [*Sir Charles and Tom retire up* C.

Mrs. H. Yes, dear, we are coming. Now, Mr. Blassy (*taking his arm*), don't forget my brother's invitation to visit us. We shall expect you. (*To Mrs. D.*) And you, Nellie, also.

Mrs. D. (*Taking Blassy's other arm.*) Certainly I shall be there. I don't propose that you shall have Mr. Blassy all to yourself. Oh, no.

[*Exeunt Blassy, Mrs. H., and Mrs. D., laughing.*

Clara. (*To Georgie.*) Well, have you got over your patriotic soreness?

Georgie. I have not, and never expect to, unless——

Clara. Unless what?

Georgie. Unless *somebody* apologizes.

Clara. Well, I dare say Sir Charles will accept an apology.

Georgie. Indeed! He will accept an apology, will he?

I want you to understand. Clara, that I consider an apology due from Sir Charles to me.

CLARA. Ah, that is quite another thing.

GEORGIE. And quite the correct thing. And I want you and your puppy English lord to know it.

CLARA. (*Petting her.*) There! there! Don't get angry—that's a little dear—and it shall receive an apology, so it shall. But suppose Sir Charles looks at it in a different light?

GEORGIE. He *mustn't* look at it in a different light.

CLARA. Oh, if he mustn't, he mustn't; and that's an end of it. When the eagle screams, let the lion beware.

GEORGIE. You may be funny if you like. But I'm going to show you that I'll bring that man to his knees, or—or he'll never see me in pa's house.

CLARA. That would be sad, indeed—too sad for contemplation. We must not permit such a catastrophe to occur. Really, the world would——

TOM. (*Turning around and moving toward the girls, Sir Charles following.*) I see the sailors are beginning to move.

SIR C. And pwaps we had bettah be doing the same.

GEORGIE. (*Aside to Clara.*) Now watch me bring that man to his knees.

CLARA. I'll watch.

GEORGIE. (*Pretending to carry on a previous conversation.*) And what a nice old gentleman he is—your father I mean, Mr. Blassy—and what a pleasant world this would be if everybody were as destitute of satirical remarks as he is.

SIR C. (*Aside to Tom.*) My boy, that is intended for me.

CLARA. I quite agree with you, Georgie. The elder Mr. Blassy is indeed a lovable old man. I could almost put my arms around his neck and call him " Father."

TOM. (*Aside to Sir C.*) Now, by Jove, *that* is intended for me.

GEORGIE. And I think it is nothing but right that people who are not entirely devoid of honor should feel sorry for words uttered that may have wounded another.

CLARA. Quite right.

GEORGIE. Then, Clara, I think you will admit that there is a gentleman around here who ought to feel sorry—and who consequently ought to apologize—for some very unkind remarks made to me.

TOM. Miss Rosewell, am I the gentleman?

GEORGIE. No, sir; you are not.

CLARA. Am I the gentleman?

GEORGIE. (*Smiling.*) Scarcely.

TOM. Why, who can it be?

GEORGIE. (*Looking demurely down at her toes.*) Is there no one else around here?

TOM. (*Looking up above his head.*) I see no one.

CLARA. (*Looking around*) Neither do I.

GEORGIE. I see you are very funny, but it is no——

SIR C. I nevah knew before that I was so attenuated as to be invisible to mortal eyes. I think Miss Wosewell wefers to me. But I was not aware that any wemarks of mine could be construed as offensive, and therefore wequiring an apology. On the contwary, I was *vewy much aware* that Miss Wosewell might with pwopriety apologize to me.

GEORGIE. Sir, your impudence is simply marvelous. Do you know to whom you speak?

SIR C. Perfectly. And to show you that I have no ill feeling, Miss Wosewell, if you will kindly specify the words that you considered personally insulting, I shall be most happy to apologize.

GEORGIE. Sir Charles Wormley, you know very well what you said. I do not now recall the particular words; but I know this, that you insulted my country, and therefore insulted me, for which I want an apology.

SIR C. Ah, that is something altogether diffewent. When your countwy demands an apology, then I will apologize to the fairest representative of your countwy.

GEORGIE. (*Sneeringly.*) To the *fairest* representative of my country?

SIR C. Yes.

GEORGIE. Hear him, Clara; he is willing to apologize to the *fairest* representative of my country. Will you please step this way?

CLARA. (*Who has been conversing aside with Tom.*) Fight your own battles, Georgie. Mr. Blassy and I are already arranging for their visit in the fall. (*Significantly.*) You'll get left if you don't mind.

GEORGIE. My sister, sir, does not want an apology. It is I who want it.

SIR C. (*Conciliatingly.*) It was you whom I meant, and it is you who shall have it.

GEORGIE. I? Then, sir, down on your—I mean, humble yourself; apologize.

SIR C. Allow me to ask first, Miss Wosewell, does your countwy wequire it?

GEORGIE. It does.

SIR C. And it is absolutely necessawy that I must obey your countwy's mandate in order to secure your forgiveness and—and good-will?

GEORGIE. It is.

SIR C. Then, come; we will talk about it. This is a vewy serious matter. (*Offers his arm.*)

GEORGIE. (*Aside, as she viciously grasps his arm.*) He has not apologized yet. I will make him do it if I have to marry him for it. [*They retire up.* L.

CLARA. (*Mockingly, aside to Georgie as they pass.*) Well, Georgie dear, did you bring him to his knees yet? Ha! ha! ha!

GEORGIE. (*In the same tone of voice.*) Not quite, Clara love; only to his arms.

CLARA. (*To Tom.*) Almost like a lovers' quarrel. Mr. Blassy; don't you think so? What do you think of it all?

TOM. I think it would be well if *we* did a little quarreling, so that you could ask me to do some apologizing

CLARA. Suppose we try?

TOM. With all my heart. But what would pa say? What would both our pa's say? They might——

GEORGIE. (*With a sudden laugh.*) How very funny you can be sometimes, Sir Charles. Clara, I am going for my wraps. Don't delay. The sailors are getting ready to drop the anchor.

[*Exeunt Georgie and Sir Charles.*

TOM. Confound it! I thought she was laughing at me.

CLARA. Then you must have a guilty conscience, Mr. Blassy. Unburden it. What were you about to say?

TOM. Only this: You said my father was a lovable old man, and that you would like—— (*A noise is heard outside.*)

CLARA. What was that?

TOM. Oh, nothing. (*Noise heard again.*)

CLARA. There it is again. They are hauling the baggage up. We must be getting ready.

TOM. The deuce take it! They are always hauling things at the wrong time. The baggage-smasher is an incubus on society. He ought to be exterminated. When he is not breaking boxes, he is breaking hearts.

[*Exeunt, arm in arm.*

The noise continues : officer on bridge gives some directions the sailors begin working the chain, and sing the following verse from the opening song :

What joy there is on a gallant bark,
 Controlled by a gallant band,
None but a fearless sailor lad
 Can ever understand,
The wild delights of a sailor's life
 'Tis useless to explain
To those who've never seen the seas,
 And crossed the Spanish Main.

Chorus.—Don't speak of pleasures of home life
  To men so bold and free.
 A sailor's life is a jovial life:
  A sailor's life for me!

While the sailors have been singing, Mr. Blassy, Mr. Rosewell, Mr. Duckerson, Sir Charles, Tom, Georgie, Clara, Mrs. Duckerson, and Mrs. Harpley have entered, carrying sachels in their hands, and wraps upon their arms.

ACT II.

SCENE 1.—*Parlor in Mr. Rosewell's house, Washington. Doors right and left, and double door center. Kate is discovered dusting.*

KATE. 'Pears to me as if Miss Georgie and Miss Clara hab neber been de same gals sence dey cum home. No singing, no dancing, no nuthin'. Always talking 'bout deir European trip, and dem lords ober dere, and old castles and abbeys and ruins. I'm sick ob it all. And den dey sometimes talk, kinder in a whisper, 'bout two fellahs dat cum ober in de same ship as dey did, and wonder why dey neber get a letter from dem. I knowed how it 'd be befo' dey went away. Says I— but here come de young ladies demselves. I must be gwine.
            [*Exit.*

Enter Georgie and Clara, C., in morning wrappers.

CLARA. Yes, yes, Georgie; I know it. Papa was only saying yesterday that it is now four weeks since we left New York, and that he thought Mr. Blassy would surely have written before this.

GEORGIE. Perhaps Mr. Blassy, the elder, is too busy seeing the sights of the great city; but I think Mr. Blassy, the younger, might have let us know if we may expect them next month.

CLARA. Yes, or Sir Charles might have——

GEORGIE. Please, Clara, don't. That man never——

CLARA. Might have written to inform us if he is yet prepared to go down on his knees. Ha! ha! ha!

GEORGIE. You are simply horrid. But he will have to apologize, even if I did apparently make it up.

CLARA. He shall.

GEORGIE. He must. And if he still——

Enter Mr. Rosewell in morning gown, slippers, etc.

MR. R. Girls, I have just received a letter from Mr. Blassy.

CLARA. (*Eagerly.*) What does he say?

GEORGIE. (*Eagerly.*) When are they coming?

MR. R. He says he has not had a spare minute, or he would have written before.

BOTH. Nothing else?

MR. R. And he says he is enjoying himself immensely, but suffering with the hot weather.

BOTH. Is that all?

MR. R. No. He also says that he is becoming, on account of the hot weather, quite thin. He knows this to be so from the fact that only a hundred boys follow him now where five hundred——

GEORGIE. Oh, pshaw! Does he say nothing about——

CLARA. He certainly has not forgotten to mention——

MR. R. (*Divining their meaning.*) Ah! yes, yes. Certainly. I see. The impatience of lovers. I ought to have known. We old men forget the callowness of youth, and the thoughts that burned within us before our beards began to sprout. Yes, in a postscript here he says the boys wrote three weeks ago, but have received no answer, and so think that they must have addressed their letters wrong. They think they must have sent them to some other Washington, as they have since learned there are about a thousand in the country. They are writing again, however, by the same mail.

GEORGIE. By the same mail?

CLARA. Where are the letters, then?

MR. R. Probably Kate has them. I will see about it, and send her in. (*Moves off, and turns suddenly.*) I have also received a letter from your Uncle George. He says the theatrical season will soon be commencing, and that he will be glad to see

us at any time. Auntie is well, and hopes the girls will not fail
to visit New York the coming fall. He incidentally mentions
that Sir Charles Wormley and Mr. Tom Blassy have called
upon him, and that he has introduced them to several lady
professionals, to whom they seem to be doing the agreeable.
But I will see Kate, and ask her about your letters. ' [*Exit.*

Georgie walks excitedly across the stage, and Clara up center.

GEORGIE.   Did you hear that—did you hear that, Clara?

CLARA.   (*With forced calmness.*)   Yes, I heard it, Georgie.

GEORGIE.   "To whom they seem to be doing the agreeable."
And still they have the audacity to write to us!

CLARA.   I suppose the next thing they will be asking us to
marry them.

GEORGIE.   (*Sneeringly.*)   And go off with them to "glorious
old England." But I wonder what they say. I wonder whether
Sir Charles writes to me or to you.

CLARA.   You don't wonder anything about it. You *know*
to whom he writes.

Enter Kate, with letters.

KATE.   Here's two letters fo' you. I forgot to bring dem in
befo'.

GEORGIE.   Please don't be so forgetful again, Kate. You
may go.   [*Exit Kate.*

Enter Mrs. Harpley, C., dressed for shopping.

MRS. H.   Dear, dear! Why, you are not ready yet. I
thought you were going shopping with me.

CLARA.   Not this morning, auntie. Georgie's head——

GEORGIE.   I do not feel quite well enough for shopping.
My head—I—I——

MRS. H.   A little fresh air would do you good, goosey.
Come, get ready—both of you.

CLARA.   No, no!

GEORGIE.   Impossible, dear auntie—impossible.

MRS. H.   Why, you stupid little creatures, what is the matter with you? It was only this morning at breakfast that you
said you would both go; that you wanted to——

CLARA.   Please, dear auntie, do leave us alone for a little
while this morning. (*Gently leads her to the door.*) We are not
in a condition—well, never mind. Good-by. (*Kisses her.*)

MRS. H.   (*Aside.*) This is very strange. Never saw them
this way before. There's something the matter, and I'm
woman enough to want to know what it is. I'll find out when

I come home. A love affair, as sure as the moon is *not* made
of green cheese. [*Exit.*

GEORGIE. (*Opening her letter.*) I thought she would never
go. It is a wonder she didn't stop half an hour just to tease us.
She knew there was something the matter. (*Reads to herself.*)

CLARA. (*Having opened her letter and read a few lines.*) Why
—why—what is this? I've actually—yes, actually got a pro-
posal.

GEORGIE. (*With a ringing laugh.*) And—and so have I.
The impudent puppy! The impudent puppy! Clara, if you
will permit me to use a little slang for once, I will remark that
this beats—Cain.

Clara walks up and down the stage, and Georgie across.

CLARA. What are you going to do about it?

GEORGIE. What are *you* going to do?

CLARA. I asked you first.

GEORGIE. Well, I don't know. It seems to me that they
are making fools of us, and love elsewhere; playing the gal-
lants to ladies in New York, and writing us what may be mock
proposals of marriage. I suppose I shall have to answer it.

CLARA. Certainly we shall have to answer. I think we
had better tell them that we can not decide until we have seen
more of them, and that we will defer our answers until they
come to see us.

GEORGIE. (*Smelling at her letter.*) This letter (*smells again*)
has had some cigar ashes on it (*smells again*) and some bad
breath near it Smell that letter, Clara, and see if it has not an
odor of stale wine.

CLARA. (*After smelling it.*) I don't smell it. Besides, I
am not sure that I know the odor of stale wine

GEORGIE. You're a dunce. Well, I smell it. This is not
my first love-letter, and I know the difference between the
smell of a cigar flavored with bad wine and the usual perfume
of a billet-doux; and if this letter has been perfumed in the
manner I assume, then the writer of it had too much wine in
him when he wrote it.

CLARA. What a preposterous supposition! I might almost
call it an asinine supposition!

GEORGIE. Not at all. Now listen, Clara; I have an idea.

CLARA. Is it possible? I always thought that giddy girls
like you, George, never had any ideas.

GEORGIE. Well, I've got one this time; and my idea is to
concoct a little plan.

CLARA. Explain.

GEORGIE. These young men may have been half drunk when they wrote these letters.

CLARA. Impossible! They are gentlemen, and gentlemen *never* get drunk.

GEORGIE. That is one of the fictions that mammas teach their good little girls.

CLARA. Why, Georgie, you are *full* of ideas. Must have been communing with your thoughts lately, an occupation new to you. Philosophers and lovers are the only ones who do that; and as you are not a philosopher, then you must be, I suppose—in love.

GEORGIE. It may be true, nevertheless.

CLARA. What, that you're in love?

GEORGIE. Goose. no. But that these young gentlemen may have been half drunk when they wrote these letters.

CLARA. But perhaps they are prohibitionists.

GEORGIE. I do not think they are. There are not many prohibitionists among the gentlemen of England.

CLARA. You seem to know a great deal about it. Sir Charles must have been quite confidential with you at some time.

GEORGIE. It did not require Sir Charles Wormley, nor even Mr. Tom Blassy, to tell me that. I could see for myself when I was over there that the English drink a great deal.

CLARA. But then they have some respect for ladies.

GEORGIE. Not much—at least, not always. I have heard that the Englishman loves his horse a little better than his dog, and his dog considerably more than his wife.

CLARA. You should not believe all that you hear. But what is your plan?

GEORGIE. My plan is this: We will go to New York as actresses seeking an engagement. We will take Uncle George into our confidence, and he shall invite (apparently unknown to us) these young gentlemen to witness a trial of our abilities. We shall then find out if they are falling in love with every girl who goes behind the footlights.

CLARA. Very good, Georgie—an excellent scheme. But don't you think they will recognize us?

GEORGIE. I'll take care of that. I'll tell Uncle George to put them behind a screen of some kind, and that they are only to hear us and not to see us. In any event, he must place us in the shade, so that, if they *should* peep (as I know they will) they can not make us out.

CLARA. But they will know our voices.

GEORGIE. Not necessarily. You know, they have never heard us sing, and that is all we shall do in their presence.

CLARA. And dance?

GEORGIE. And dance, of course, in a mild way. And if we should have to speak a few words, why we can disguise our voices.

CLARA. But what will pa and auntie say?

GEORGIE. Oh, we shall have to tell them that we are going on a visit to Uncle George

CLARA. Which, of course, we shall be doing; and so we shall not be telling a story.

GEORGIE. Certainly, certainly. It would not do to tell a story. Lovers *never* tell stories. They always——

CLARA. Why, here's auntie back from shopping.

Enter Mrs. Harpley with three or four parcels, which she lays on the table.

GEORGIE. And, unlike us, she is full of good sense and—other things.

MRS. H. Yes, and other things. Just look here. (*Attempts to undo a parcel.*) See what I've been buying while you two geese have been talking love and such stuff.

CLARA. What is it, auntie—a yard of tape?

GEORGIE. Or a spool of thread—which?

MRS. H. It is neither, you goslings. I knew I should make your eyes water. Look! It is a duck of a bonnet. (*Exhibits a bonnet.*)

CLARA Oh, what a beauty! Isn't it handsome?

GEORGIE. It's just too lovely for anything! Did you buy it for me, auntie? It will just match——

CLARA. Do let me try it on.

MRS. H. (*Picking up her parcels.*) Come, both of you. I want to show you something else—something you've never seen before. Oh, it's simply grand.

GEORGIE. What is it? What is it? What is it?

CLARA. Oh, do tell, auntie! Do tell!

MRS. H. Not now, dears. Wait until we get upstairs. Come.

BOTH GIRLS. Oh, what is it, auntie? What is it? What is it?

Exeunt; Mrs. H. carrying her parcels, and Georgie and Clara hugging her.

SCENE 2.—*The Bowery, New York City. A dog barking is heard outside, and a noise as though the dog were worrying something. Enter John Blassy backwards slowly, and trying to kick the dog off, which he succeeds in doing just as he comes on. His trousers are disarranged, his hat awry, and he is panting for breath.*

BLASSY. Save, me, lads! Save me! I am worried by dogs. (*Gives a kick. Looks, and sees there is no dog there.*) Now, by the fat of all my ancestors, I know not why that dog should treat me thus. I was walking quietly along the Bowery just now when that skulking pup, that dirt-enveloped cur, that hungry-looking hound, that flea-devoured mongrel, that yelping, snarling, crust-eating snipe of the gutter, flew at me from behind a boy's legs, and attacked my extremities most villainously. I did not hear the lad say anything to the dog, nor did I see the dog wink to the lad; hence I am at a loss to account for it. H'm, now I think on't, I've heerd that here in New York dogs are taught to know a Chinaman, and to fly at him on sight. But am I a Chinaman? Bah! (*Takes out his handkerchief.*) Do I look like one? Bah! (*Wipes his face.*) True, I am shrinking away. This hot weather is having its effect. I am becoming a mere shadow of my former self. Another month of it, and I shall be as lean and wizened as one of Duckerson's professional skeletons. But I am not becoming mooneyed. Nay, lads, I am not becoming moon-eyed, am I? (*Looks up to the gallery.*) This is frightful! This is frightful! An honest British merchant to be taken for a rat-eating Mongolian. Does *this* come from eating rats? (*Puts his hands on his stomach.*) Nay, I think not; but good beef, lads—juicy beef and ale. My mishaps in this great city have been many; but to be taken for a Chinaman is the unkindest one of all. I shall write a book when I go home. Everybody does it It pays—so I've heerd. And I shall have lots to say about the gamins. They do not follow me so much as they did, which is one reason why I think I am getting thin. Occasionally they seize upon me, and then —yes, then I have a frightful time. For a week or two after I landed I could not leave my hotel without an army of small boys following me. Some would whisper (as only small boys can whisper): "Have a care, old man; if you fall, the earth will quake." Others would shout: "How much fur yer beetle-crushers, Mr. Shadow?" I have since learned they meant my boots; I wear No. 15's. Still others would yell—— (*A noise is heard outside.*) Ah, here's a crowd of 'em coming now. I had better be going, methinks.

Enter, before Blassy can get away, about ten Bowery boys. One shouts, "Here's old Anti-fat!" They immediately surround Blassy. Four get hold of his coat-tails and pull him different ways. Another four jump around him and keep up a hideous noise. One crawls between his legs, and as he emerges exclaims, "Oh, what a Jumbo foot!" Another jumps on his shoulder and yells in his ear: "Where are yer now, old Lamp-post? Old Beef-eater, where are yer now? What'll yer gimme to let up on yer, old Plum-pudding?" While Blassy is making a vigorous effort to shake the boys off, Sir Charles and Tom Blassy enter: whereupon the boys run off.

BLASSY. (*In a weak voice, overcome with fatigue.*) This is frightful! This is frightful! (*A little louder.*) I can not stand this much longer. My life is a burden.

TOM. (*Disgustedly.*) Or your burden is your life.

BLASSY. All the ragamuffins in the land follow me with cries of "Anti-fat!"

TOM. They ought to follow you with cries of "Fatty Auntie!"

BLASSY. (*Brushing and arranging his clothes.*) This is a beastly country, where an *honest* man is a curiosity or a subject of mirth.

SIR C. It is not for your honesty, Mr. Bwassy, that the boys honah you with their notice, but for your excessive corpulency.

BLASSY. I say it is for my honesty—my excessive honesty; for no man gets fat who is not honest. And a country that has no fat men has no honest men.

SIR C. But Amewica has thousands of fat men.

BLASSY. Indeed! Then she *must* have some honest men.

Enter George Duckerson in time to hear the last remark. He is dressed in a light summer suit, and has a brisk air about him. He slaps Blassy familiarly.

DUCK. Right you are, old man; right you are. We're not all bank cashiers. But how's your good health? (*Shakes his hand.*) Mrs. D. will be here in a minute; just dropped into a store to buy some—some candy, I believe. And how's the kids? (*Turns around and shakes a hand each of Sir Charles and Tom.*) Blooming, I see. Never better. Ha! ha! ha! (*Pokes them both in the ribs significantly.*)

SIR C. The kids are well, thank you.

Tom. And are enjoying themselves immensely.

Duck. I know it; I know it. Have heard all about your pretty doings lately. By Cain, but you are going it lively for two—two greenies. Ha! ha! ha! (*Turns to Blassy.*) And how's the hot weather skinning your bones now, old Broadsides? Still the same old thing, I see. Still good for a show. How about my proposition? Did you think of it? Consider my offer still open. I'm just out for——

Mrs. D. (*In the wings.*) You old, impatient, unfeeling wretch, you! (*Enter.*) Not even one minute can you wait till I—— (*Becomes all smiles upon seeing Mr Blassy.*) Ah, Mr. Blassy, so glad to see you (*Shakes his hand heartily.*) I was just scolding Mr. Duckerson for leaving me; but I see he has got into better company. Why, what makes you frown so? Has he been saying something dreadful?

Blassy. Not very dreadful, but very irritating. He needs a lashing, Mrs. Duckerson. He needs a woman's tongue.

Mrs. D. If that is all the lashing he needs, I may say he gets it quite often.

Blassy. Apparently not often enough.

Mrs. D. Didn't you hear the sample I gave him just now?

Blassy. Why, look you, Mrs Duckerson, I am myself somewhat acquainted with the endearments of matrimony; and that was a mere matrimonial endearment compared to what he should get.

Mrs. D. Oh, I don't know what I shall do; I really don't. He's perfectly awful—perfectly awful. But how's your son and Sir Charles? (*Turns to them.*)

Sir C. Speaking for myself, Mrs. Duckerson, nevah bettah.

Tom. And I have nothing serious to complain about

Duck. Now, Nellie dear, vacate. We three have a little business to talk about.

Mrs. D. I'll go when I please, George.

Duck. That's a good wifey; I know you will. So please to go, and here's the pound of chocolate creams I promised you. (*Attempts to snatch a kiss, but she prevents him.*)

Mrs. D. Viper, how dare you?

Duck. Talk to old Longbottom there; he's waiting for you.

Mrs. D. Come, Mr. Blassy, you shall be my escort this afternoon.

Blassy. (*Looking pleased.*) To—to what do I owe this unlooked-for pleasure?

Mrs. D. Oh, George has got a little business with Sir Charles and your son.

BLASSY. But—but are you not—not afraid, you know, to walk with me?

MRS D. Why should I be afraid to walk with you, Mr. Blassy?

BLASSY. My—my extraordinary size, you know. Boys will be boys, and they sometimes insult me.

MRS. D. They will not insult you if I'm with you.

BLASSY. Why so?

MRS. D. They never insult gentlemen who are with ladies.

BLASSY. Very extraordinary country where the ladies protect the gentlemen—very extraordinary. I thought it was a universal rule for gentlemen to protect the ladies.

MRS D Well, you see, the ladies in my country have some rights that everybody is bound to respect; and that is one of them. Wearing large Gainsborough hats at the theater is another, and the poor men dare not say anything. (*She takes his arm.*) Take care of yourselves, gentlemen. (*To Sir C., Tom, and Mr. D.*) We are going for a walk.

> [*Exeunt Mr. Blassy and Mrs. D., talking quite lovingly together.*

DUCK Well, boys, how did you like the lay-out—the little dainties I spread before you?

TOM. Hugely.

SIR C. Gawgeous cweatures! Gawgeous! Gawgeous!

DUCK. Ha! ha! ha! I told you they were fine girls. I suppose you took them out again yesterday?

TOM. Yes; and we have planned another drive for to-morrow.

DUCK. By Moses! but you are wiping the town up lively!

SIR C. Won't you join us to-mowow with that other chawming cweature, Mrs. Duckerson?

DUCK Couldn't possibly do it; have a business engagement.

SIR C. A what?

DUCK. A business engagement.

TOM. (*Incredulously.*) That will do, Duckerson. We know something about *your* business engagements.

DUCK. You may believe me or not, gentlemen; but two ladies of the profession wish to see me to-morrow.

SIR C. A vewy pwetty story.

TOM Full of ingenuity and—and truthfulness.

DUCK. It's a fact, boys. Seeking an engagement, I believe, and wish to give me a specimen of their talent. They——

SIR C. Ha! ha! ha! Capital!

Tom.   The story further embellished and rounded out

Sir C.   Give it another touch, Duckerson.

Tom.   Yes.   The story lacks finish.

Duck.   You don't believe me!   All right.   Good day.
(*Turns to go.*)

Sir C.   Here stop, Duckerson.   If your story is twue, what
say you to giving us a peep at these new beauties?

Duck.   Couldn't possibly do it   Wouldn't think of it.

Tom.   Our drive for to-morrow could be postponed, you
know.

Duck.   I tell you I couldn't think of it.   My professional
reputation would be at stake.   I could never——

Sir C.   The deuce take your pwofessional weputation.

Duck.   I could never look——

Tom.   You could easily get us into the room, put us behind
some screen, and the thing is done.

Duck.   Boys, you take my breath away.   You make me
gasp.

Sir C.   If you want us to believe your vewy ingenious
womance, you see how you can do it.

Tom.   Come now, what say you, Ducky, old boy?

Duck.   (*Reluctantly.*)   Well, I don't know—I don't know.
Perhaps I might manage it.   But it hurts me—it hurts my professional pride.

Sir C.   Well, if that is all that will get hurt, vewy few people will know it, and still fewer will believe it.

Duck.   Suppose the girls should see or hear you?

Tom.   We'll watch that.   Our applause shall be confined to
a gurgle of admiration.

Duck.   You promise not to show yourselves, nor to beg for
an introduction?

Sir C.   We pwomise on our honah.

Duck.   Then, if you're determined upon it, be at my office
to-morrow at half-past two, or a little before.   Good day, and
be very careful of yourselves.   (*Aside*)   I hooked my fish that
time.

Sir C. and Tom.   Good day.   Good day.

[*Exit Duckerson*, R.

Sir C.   Capital! capital!   More worlds to conquer.

Tom.   But that was a mustard plaster—not to beg for an
introduction.

Sir C.   Aw, well.   Things will adjust themselves in time.

Tom.   I fear not in our time.   Look who is coming.

Enter Blassy and Mrs. Duckerson still arm in arm, but Blassy is puffing and almost out of breath

BLASSY. My spleen! My spleen!

MRS. D. I'm really sorry, Mr. Blassy, if I have been walking too fast for you.

BLASSY. Not at all. Don't worry It'll be over in a minute.

SIR C. What, back alweady?

MRS. D. Yes, and we have had a splendid walk. Been all down the Bowery, along Canal Street, Grand Street, Bleecker Street, up Broadway——

TOM. No wonder my father is blowing like a porpoise.

SIR C. Mrs. Duckerson has only been exercising him a little—twaining him, perhaps, for some pugilistic contest.

BLASSY. It's nothing, boys. Nothing—nothing.

SIR C. Or for some future gladiatowial exhibition with the Bowery small boy. Now twy the dumb-bells.

MRS. D. Ha! ha! ha! Yes, Mr. Blassy has been telling me all about it; how you rescued him from the jaws of—the very jaws of death. How dreadful it must be to be fleshy. But where is my husband?

SIR C. Gone—gone home. (*Aside.*) I pwesume.

MRS. D. Gone home? Then I must be going too, and be there before him, or I shall never hear the last of my escapade with Father Blassy. Ha! ha! ha!

SIR C. Don't be in a hurwy. Shall one of us accompany you home?

MRS. D. No, thank you; I'd rather go alone. Good-by. Ta-ta, Mr. Blassy.

Blassy kisses his hand, and the others say "Good-by."

[*Exit Mrs. Duckerson.*

BLASSY. A charming woman, but fear—fearfully fast. (*Hastening to correct himself.*) I mean a fearfully fast walker.

TOM. Father, you're a chump.

BLASSY. A what, me lad?

TOM. A chump.

BLASSY. What is a chump?

TOM. Well, if I must tell you, it is slang for a blockhead, a dolt, a fool.

BLASSY. Tom, Tom, me lad, don't call your old father a fool. Call me a blockhead, a dolt, a jackass, an' you will; but call me not a fool.

Tom. I did not mean to call you a fool, father. A "chump" is not quite so expressive as that. It means a person who has *acted* foolishly. And you act foolishly, father, in indulging in the pleasures of the table so much when you see that it keeps you so fat. It nettles me to see my old father the sport of boys, when he might, by a little self-denial, reduce his size to that of ordinary mortals, and thereby prevent his being a jest forever

Blassy. Aye, aye, me lad; but how?

Sir C. 'hat's it, Mr. Bwassy. How?

Tom. Live on bread and water, if there's no other way.

Blassy. Well, well, Tom; we'll not quarrel. When you get to my age, you will learn that it is no easy thing to live on bread and water.

Sir C. 'Tis even worse, I should judge, than wiving on bread and cheese and kisses.

Tom. He might try the kisses alone. Some people live on love.

Sir C. Or dyspepsia. Dyspepsia is a never-failing wemedy with Americans for reducing flesh. Try and get dyspepsia.

Blassy. What is dyspepsia, Sir Charles?

Sir C. Dyspepsia? Why anybody in this countwy can tell you what dyspepsia is.

Blassy. Do they sell it in drug stores?

Sir C. In some dwug stores—yes.

Blassy. And you are sure it is a good remedy?

Sir C. Perfectly sure.

Blassy. Ever try it yourself?

Sir C. Nevah.

Blassy. Then how do you know it is good?

Sir C. I judge fwom its effects on the specimens I have seen.

Blassy. I'll get some! I'll get some!

Sir C. Then I'll have to intwoduce you to some sufferwing native. He'll show you how to take it.

Blassy. Sir Charles, I'm your devoted friend. Show me how to take dyspepsy, and I'm your devoted slave.

Sir C. All you have to do is to watch him at the table. He takes it at his meals.

Blassy. (*All moving off together.*) Before or after?

Sir C. Sometimes before, but generally after.

Blassy. I'll buy some, Sir Charles; I'll buy some. I'll try dyspepsy. I'll try it! I'll try it! Anything to reduce this Rocky Mountain of flesh.

                                    [*Exeunt.*

SCENE 3.—*Mr. Duckerson's office in his theater. Enter Mr. Duckerson.*

DUCK. (*Looking at his watch.*) It is now twenty minutes after two. I told Sir Charles and Tom to be here a little before half past. They have not the faintest suspicion of who the ladies are, and I do not intend that they shall be enlightened. I suppose they will go wild, and want presenting this very afternoon. Oh, no. I shall hustle the girls into a carriage immediately after it's over, and the young fellows may rave themselves sick. It's only fun for the girls, I know; but I've given my word of honor to do this thing squarely, and I mean to do it. It may be that they—(*a knock is heard*)—ah, here they are. Come in.

Enter Sir Charles and Tom Blassy.

DUCK. (*Continuing.*) How do, gentlemen? Just in time. Beaten the ladies by a neck. Now don't break your necks in beating them behind that screen. Let me——

TOM. Now this is no hoax.

SIR C. Nor one of your infernal jokes?

DUCK. Never more serious in my life. I'm trembling in my boots. Wish I hadn't let you come.

TOM. Ducky, old boy, you won't refuse us now.

SIR C. Wemember, Duckerson, we know a pwetty little story about you that Mrs. Duckerson——

DUCK. Well, then, hurry up. Here, get behind this screen. I hear the ladies coming. Hurry—hurry! (*He pushes them partly behind the screen.*)

TOM. One moment. Suppose—suppose—oh, hang it! Sir Charles, you say it.

SIR C. I think Tom is twying to say, Mr. Duckerson, that if we should take a particular fancy to these wadies, you surely would not wefuse——

DUCK. Don't have time to listen. (*A knock is heard at the door.*) Now be slippery. Look lively. Get behind there. (*He pushes them again.*) Come in

Enter Georgie and Clara dressed in elegant style, but contrasting somewhat, each with parasol, gloves, etc.

GEORGIE. (*In a disguised voice.*) This is the manager, I believe?

DUCK. (*Bowing.*) It is, at your service.

CLARA. (*In a disguised voice.*) And you received our letter, I presume?

DUCK. I did.

GEORGIE. Aw, then we will proceed to business without further ceremony.

DUCK. May I ask what line of business?

CLARA. A little of everything.

GEORGIE. Down to song and dance.

DUCK. Indeed! I should be pleased to witness a trial of your abilities as song and dance artistes.

CLARA. Certainly.

GEORGIE. (*Whispering.*) Are they here, uncle?

DUCK. (*Whispering.*) Yes; behind that screen there. But don't speak so loud.

GEORGIE. (*Moving toward the screen.*) We have scarcely room here, Mr. Duckerson. Suppose we move——

DUCK. Don't kick that screen, ladies. (*Sir C. and Tom start in surprise.*)

CLARA. It takes up too much room. If you will kindly——

DUCK. I tell you again, ladies, don't kick that screen.

GEORGIE. We are not going to kick it, sir. We are only going to move it.

CLARA. I think the gentleman must have something behind the screen that he does not wish us to see. He seems so anxious about it.

GEORGIE. Perhaps a bull-dog. (*Clara screams.*)

DUCK. Yes, I have a bull-dog there—two of 'em. (*Both ladies scream.*) And British bull-dogs at that. (*Both scream again, and Sir C and Tom shake their fists angrily.*) Fighting bull-dogs—vicious, snarling beasts. So look out, and don't go too near.

CLARA. Oh, Mr. Duckerson, Mr. Duckerson, why did you allow us to come here?

GEORGIE. We had no idea that this was a menagerie. Have you any other wild beasts? (*Sir C. and Tom start again at the thought of being compared to wild beasts.*)

DUCK. No others, I assure; and these bull-dogs won't hurt you if you keep out of their way. Besides, they're chained up, and I've put a muzzle on them.

CLARA. Put a muzzle on them?

DUCK. You bet. I've got 'em where the hair is short.

CLARA. Then how do they eat?

DUCK. Oh, like dogs. (*Sir C. and Tom gleam with rage.*)

GEORGIE. But how do you feed them?

DUCK. Feed them sometimes with my boot, but oftener with a club.

CLARA. Don't you give them anything else?

DUCK. Not much else during the dog-days, and we are now in the dog-days. At least, they are in *their* dog-days. Every dog has his day.

TOM. (*To Sir C.*) I will not stand this much longer.

SIR C. (*To Tom*) He's a villainous mountebank. I shall take the wiberty of pulling his nose at the first opportunity.

GEORGIE. You seem to know a great deal about dogs.

DUCK. About bull-dogs—yes. But these are only puppies. At least, I don't think they are full-grown, because they have such puppy ways.

CLARA. Oh, why then we needn't be afraid of them.

DUCK. Not a bit. They're really the most harmless puppies you ever saw. They think they've lots of courage, like all puppies, but they haven't a thimbleful. They crawl into their holes on the slightest scent of danger. They crawled into their present holes because they heard a footstep on the stairs.

TOM. (*To Sir C.*) This is horrible!

SIR C. (*To Tom.*) Most horwibly horwible! A Bwitish peer cwawling into a hole to be the sport of a knavish show-man.

GEORGIE How I should like one.

DUCK. What, one of these?

GEORGIE. No, no; I didn't mean that.

CLARA. She meant a bull-pup like one of these.

DUCK. Oh, well; perhaps I'll make you a present of one of these some day. But let me show you them. They are fine specimens. Just one peep. (*Sir C. and Tom fall back in dismay.*)

BOTH GIRLS. Oh, no, no, no.

GEORGIE. I'm afraid of their fangs.

CLARA. I can almost see their gleaming eye-balls.

DUCK. All right. As you say. We'll take a peep at them some other time—when they're asleep, perhaps.

GEORGIE. That will be better.

DUCK. Well, then, let us to business. What will you try?

GEORGIE. We have had written for us a little song of the sea that we will try.

DUCK. All right. That will remind us of those other dogs—the sea-dogs.

CLARA. Exactly.

DUCK. Well, then, all ready?

GEORGIE All ready.

They sing and dance the following :

OLD OCEAN.

Glorious sea !   Boundless sea !
How delightful to be
Rocked to sleep by thy leonine hand,
In forgetful repose
Of the world and its woes !
For all ills fly away at thy wand.

What on earth can compare
With thy rich bracing air
For the poor weary toilers of earth ?
Yielding health, yielding wealth,
Doing good e'en by stealth,
Asking naught in exchange for thy worth.

Land is bought ; land is sold ;
Men bequeath men its gold ;
But no birthright thou ever hast known.
All to thee are the same :
Rich and poor, strong and lame,
Can inherit thee and call thee their own.

Let us go, then, away, .
To the beach, where the spray
Murmurs sweetly its song of the sea ;
And we'll sit on the shore,
Watch the waves dash and roar,
Dreaming sadly, Old Ocean, of thee.

ACT III.

SCENE 1.—*Grounds and conservatory around Mr. Rosewell's
house, Washington.   Three rustic seats partially concealed from
each other.   Enter John Blassy, arm in arm with Mrs. Harpley
and Mrs. Duckerson.   Blassy is in full evening dress, a little
old-fashioned—large double-breasted white vest and large neck-tie.*

BLASSY.   (*Wiping his forehead.*)   'Pears to me you have dinner early in this country.   In my——

MRS. H.   We consider it good for digestion.

BLASSY.   But my digestion is very good.

MRS. H.   But not very complete.   I mean——

MRS. D.   Exactly what you say, Alice.   Mr. Blassy's digestion is not very complete, else he would not be so fleshy.

BLASSY.   Why, my dears, I am taking physic to cure that. But more physic I take, the more I seem to eat.   Didn't you notice my appetite at dinner?

MRS. H.   Not particularly.

MRS. D.   We all eat rather heartily, I thought.

BLASSY.   But my appetite is—is frightful—frightful.   Howsomever, I am taking physic for it.   I am taking dyspepsy—I think Sir Charles calls it.   Funny name.   (*Both ladies look at each other in blank astonishment.*)   Never heard of it in my life before.

MRS. H.   What did you say the medicine was, Mr. Blassy?

BLASSY.   Dyspepsy—yes, dyspepsy.   I'm cartain that's the name.

MRS. D.   He *must* mean dyspepsia.

MRS H.   But taking it as a medicine.   I don't understand. Do you buy this medicine?

BLASSY.   Why bless my 'art, yes.   Buy it in a drug-store. Dollar and a quarter a bottle; six bottles for——   (*Both ladies burst into peals of laughter.*)   I—I see nothing funny about it. Cost me twenty-four dollars already.   And now——

MRS. D.   Who told you of this medicine?

BLASSL.   Sir Charles—Sir Charles did.   He said it was a capital thing for reducing flesh.   Nearly every American took it.

MRS. D.   (*Slyly.*)   It doesn't seem to reduce *your* flesh, much, Mr. Blassy.

MRS. H.   Sir Charles told you!   I didn't think that of Sir Charles—didn't think he was such a wag   Now if it had been your husband, Nellie, I could have understood it.

MRS D.   Yes, indeed.   If it had been George, the thing would have been perfectly consistent   But Sir Charles——

BLASSY.   Bless your 'arts, ladies, what do you mean?   I'm all at sea.   They both told me.   I never——

BOTH LADIES   (*Bursting into laughter again.*)   'Tis enough! 'Tis enough!

BLASSY.   Some joke on me, I'll bet a sovereign.   I've been the victim of waggery ever since I landed in the country. Booming queer country!   Every man a joker, and every joker taking physic.

MRS. D.   But how did George come to tell you that dyspepsia was good for reducing flesh?

BLASSY.   Why the way on't was this: Sir Charles told me
that I should watch some suffering native taking it at his meals.
With that he took me over to Mr. Duckerson, who was just
eating dinner, and told him what I wanted.   Now I think on't,
he *did* seem a little staggered; but he immediately got up and
said: "Ah, yes, yes.   I have a bottle of it here.   I take mine
before meals; some take it after, and some take it all the time.
I would advise you to take it all the time, John.   It's very fine
stuff—very fine stuff.   Try it.   Costs only a dollar and a quarter
a bottle."   I did try it.   It tasted very good   It had a suspi-
cious flavor of port wine.   I liked it all the better   After dinner he took me to the only druggist in town, as he said, where I
could get it.

MRS. H.   And you bought a bottle?

BLASSY.   Six of 'em.   Because, you see, I take it all the time.

MRS. D.   But what did the druggist say when you inquired
for a bottle of dyspepsia?

BLASSY.   H'm.   Ah.   Now I remember he did smile a little.
But I thought nothing on't at the time.   Duckerson told him I
wanted it like his, and then whispered a few words which I
failed to catch.   The druggist then asked, "Will one bottle be
enough?" and Duckerson said, "Take six, John; take six."
So I took six.   Have been taking six ever since.   But it seems
I get fatter.

MRS. H.   Did you bring any with you to Washington, Mr.
Blassy?

BLASSY.   Brought six bottles when I came a week ago, but
it's nearly all gone.   I shall have to send for more.

MRS. D.   Any about your person now?

BLASSY.   Yes, I always keep a small bottle about me.   Will
you taste it?   (*Produces a bottle.*)

MRS. D.   Certainly.   (*They both taste it.*)

Enter Mr. Duckerson and Mr. Rosewell, C.

BLASSY.   It has a very good flavor.   Don't be afraid of it.
I drink a bottle a day of it sometimes.

DUCK.   (*Aside to Mr. Rosewell*)   Zounds, Robert!   Look at
that, will you?   Look at that!   Old Broadsides carries his
bottle of brandy with him, and induces ladies to drink in secret
out of the same bottle.   By heavens, and my wife, too!

MR. R.   This is very strange of Mr. Blassy.

DUCK.   Hello there!   What's all this about?   My wife

drinking whisky in secret? And you, Alice, also? I thought *you* had more respect for yourself. I know my wife is capable of anything, but you—I——

MRS. D. You miserable, horrid wretch, you! You ought to be flogged! This is some of *your* whisky—some of *your* medicine—*your* cure for fat (*Duckerson begins to realize* **what is** *the matter, smiles, and finally bursts into a loud guffaw*), that only *your* druggist is able to supply poor Mr. Blassy here at a dollar and a quarter a bottle For shame!

MR. R. (*To Blassy, taking hold of his arm.*) Some dreadful joke, I see, of my brother-in law. Pray excuse him, Mr. Blassy; pray excuse him He is never happy but when he is funny, and never funny but when he is happy. (*They retire up* c., *Blassy shaking his head dubiously.*) Let it pass. You have two able defenders in my sisters

DUCK. My sweet chicken, my adorable ranter, you are too severe John will bear me out that——

MRS. D. And pray who is John? You do not mean——

DUCK. Who is John? Why, old Anti-fat there

MRS. H. I'm perfectly ashamed of you, George. To speak that way of a guest in my brother's house.

> *Enter Sir Charles and Georgie, who sit on one of the rustic*
> *seats; then follow Tom and Clara, who take another seat.*

MRS. D. And one worth ten of you.

DUCK. He will *weigh* ten of me if he goes on taking my medicine.

MRS. D. Viper! I have no patience!

DUCK. I am miserably aware of it, my dear.

> *Mrs. D. walks across the stage, too angry to speak.*

MRS. H. What will Mr. Blassy think of us? What will he think of American ladies and gentlemen? What will he do when he gets home?

DUCK. He'll write a book, and put me in as the chief comic character—next to himself.

MRS. H. George, have you *no* reason? Do you never get into a thoughtful mood?

MRS. D. He never does, Alice; he never does. Let us go. I am sick. An eternally funny man is the greatest bore in existence.

DUCK. Yes, let us go; let us go look at the ducks. In the meantime I will offer you each a wing. (*He offers them his arms.*)

MRS. H. There he goes again with his buffoonery.

MRS. D. And truly he is only a buffoon, and a disgusting one at that. (*They take his arm, and move off.*)

DUCK I am always obliging to ladies. If a wing is not sufficient, then take the whole duck. (*He clasps them both suddenly around the waist, and exeunt in that position*)

MR. R. (*To Blassy.*) No, I'm afraid we shall not get the bill through this session. But don't let that worry you

BLASSY. It *does* worry me. I am going home in a month.

MR. R. Not so soon, Mr. Blassy; not so soon. Why, you haven't seen any of the wonders of our great country yet. You haven't even seen any of our Indians, our Congressmen, and other—and other wild tribes.

BLASSY. Ha! ha! ha! Never thought of it. Where can I see them?

MR R. Many of them—our Congressmen, for instance—you can see there on Capitol Hill, in the Cave of the Winds.

BLASSY. Cave of the Winds—Cave of the Winds.

MR. R. Yes; or Windy Cave.

BLASSY. Windy Cave. Why Windy Cave?

MR R. Oh, because it is so very windy up there when the average Congressman is spouting.

BLASSY. Ha! ha! ha! You Americans *are* a 'umerous lot; you *are* a 'umerous lot

MR. R It often blows so hard that nobody but his constituents ever hear what he says.

BLASSY Ha! ha! ha! Ha! ha! ha! All jokers—all jokers.   [*Exeunt Mr. Rosewell and Mr. Blassy.*

Tom and Clara rise slowly from their seats.

CLARA. (*Plucking a flower.*) Only a rosebud. Pretty, is it not?

TOM. Yes, very

CLARA. Are you fond of rosebuds?

TOM. Of *that* rosebud, yes.

CLARA. I would put it in your button-hole, but I'm afraid.

TOM. Afraid? Why?

CLARA. Oh, I don't know if you don't.

TOM. Well, I'm sure I don't. So put it there.

CLARA. But what would some of those New York ladies say?

TOM. (*Startled.*) What do you mean?

CLARA. Oh, I don't know if you don't.

TOM. I fail to penetrate. Is that why you are afraid?

CLARA. Yes.

TOM. Then be not afraid any longer. Put it there.

CLARA. (*Putting it in his button-hole.*) But you might think too much of it.

TOM. I couldn't.

CLARA. But you might.

TOM. Impossible.

CLARA. There! It looks decidedly æsthetic on its background of black.

TOM. May I think as much of it as I like?

CLARA. Oh, yes; a flower means nothing. But I told you I was afraid you would think too much of it.

TOM. I can never do that. What do you call this cluster that you wear in your—in your corsage, is it? I'm not well versed in women's dress.

CLARA. You will be some day.

TOM. What do you mean?

CLARA. When you marry. Your check-book will enlighten you.

TOM. (*Putting his arm lightly around her waist.*) If money could buy such a thing of beauty as this, then——

CLARA. (*Gently disengaging herself.*) That will do. Don't carry my joke too far.

TOM. Is it very expensive?

CLARA. What?

TOM. A wife.

CLARA. I don't think so. But I've never been a wife.

TOM. Quite right. I didn't think of that. But you might be some day.

CLARA. I hope so, though I don't think I have seen my husband yet.

TOM. Are you sure?

CLARA. I see plenty of gentlemen I like, but few that——I have no heart, I'm afraid.

TOM. I'm afraid you have not.

CLARA. What do you know about it?

TOM. A good deal. I have been looking for it.

CLARA. You are as foolish as all the rest. I don't like men who can talk nothing but nonsense.

TOM. It is not nonsense. Men sometimes mean what they say.

CLARA. Very rarely. Do you remember our first meeting?

TOM. No. I know it was on shipboard; but our acquaintance never seems to have had a beginning. I simply *knew* you.

CLARA. And trusted me?

TOM. And trusted you.

CLARA.   My! I don't know.   It was not ——

TOM.   What?

CLARA.   Never mind.   Did you like New York?

TOM.   Will you not finish your sentence?

CLARA.   It was nothing—a thought that should not have been uttered anyway.   But tell me, are you going back to London?

TOM.   Yes, I suppose it is best for me.

CLARA.   I suppose—it—is.

TOM.   I fear I shall not be happy, though.

CLARA.   Yes, you will.   There's where the eyes of the world are centered.   There's where there is brilliancy, and gayety, and clever people, and worldly power; and you will find another—I mean other friends.

TOM.   And so you wish me happiness?

CLARA.   Indeed—indeed, I do.

TOM.   Then why not contribute towards it?

CLARA.   Tell me how I can.   I will do anything within my power.   We have talked frankly enough at times; let us talk frankly now.

TOM.   Our friendship has been wasted if we can not be frank with each other now.   I am going away soon

CLARA.   Yes, you are going away soon.   To say that I shall miss you is to talk platitudes.   I dare not speak what I feel. You will not misunderstand me?

TOM.   No; you may be sure of that.

CLARA.   You need not squeeze my hand quite so hard.

TOM.   Did I really have hold of your hand?   I was thinking—— (*Slight pause.*)

CLARA.   Well, of what were you thinking?

TOM.   I have never (*looking at her dubiously*)—I have never spoken of love.   Sometimes a little sentiment has stolen in, but you have not encouraged it, not even——

CLARA.   I don't like sentiment.   It's always hollow and foolish.

TOM.   But have you not sometimes thought I loved you?

CLARA.   Yes, sometimes.   And I shouldn't wonder if you have not sometimes thought I loved *you.*

TOM.   I have, sometimes.

CLARA.   But how could I love a man who never sought to be anything but a friend?

TOM.   And how could I ask a woman who gave me her friendship to accept my love as a reward for her friendship, and to give me hers as a reward for mine?   If I had taken advantage of your friendship to make love to you, I should have come to the base level of the rest of mankind.

CLARA. Now you are talking nonsense. Do you believe that I would ever have given you my confidence if there had been nothing but friendship? And I am very much mistaken if friendship ever could be so warm as yours that had no deeper motive power.

TOM. Take care, Clara; you are committing yourself.

CLARA. Committing myself or not, why should I not speak in a matter that so nearly concerns my happiness? Tom, you are going away; you are going to leave me; you have taught me to trust you; you have weaned me from all other confidants, and made me one-half of yourself You have known all the time that I loved you. If I have read you wrongly, it has not been your fault. Our happiness calls for us to speak the truth —woman or man.

TOM. Clara, you have read me aright, as I have you. No woman that had not all my love could have had all my friendship, as you have had. You are my other self; and where I go, you shall go. I believe that we were made one for the other. (*Kisses her.*)

CLARA. And now, Tom, darling, I don't mind if you do indulge in a little sentiment now

TOM. (*Encircling her waist very lovingly.*) And nonsense, too?

CLARA. And nonsense, too.

TOM. (*Kissing her again.*) This kind of nonsense?

CLARA. Yes.

They move up the stage very fondly, and come suddenly upon Mr. Blassy and Mrs. Harpley, who have just entered.

BLASSY. (*Disgustedly.*) Drat it! Drat it! These young 'uns are always so intent upon their own love-making that they never see anybody else.

MRS. H. Why you were not making love, Mr. Blassy. Why should you be annoyed?

BLASSY. I am not annoyed, Mrs. Harpley. But I was— well, I can't express—I mean I was—I was *feeling* love, if I was not *making* love.

MRS. H. Pshaw! Mr. Blassy. Pshaw! A man of your age.

BLASSY. Why, look you, Mrs. Harpley, my vigor is not yet affected by my age, and my age is not so great as to have weakened my constitution, and my constitution is good for another thirty years.

MRS H. (*Edging a little closer to him.*) But what has all that to do with me?

Sir Charles and Georgie get up and move slowly toward the footlights, unconscious of Blassy and Mrs. H.

BLASSY. Why, look you, only this: I have been thinking lately what is life worth living for if not to—in short, I have been a widower now some—— Drat the infernal luck! Drat it! Here's another spoony couple! Always coming when I am in a mellow mood, and want to say something—but come, come.   [*Mrs. H. takes his arm, and exeunt talking together*

SIR C. This is not spwingtime, is it, Miss Wosewell?

GEORGIE. Certainly not.

SIR C. Then I'm sure there must be something in the Amewican climate conducive to love and tender thoughts. A fellow seems to dwop as natuwally into love as—as—I beg pardon, Miss Wosewell, but am I not getting foolish?

GEORGIE. Perhaps you are. But I—but *I* do not think so. Pray go on, Sir Charles.

SIR C. (*Toying with his eye-glass.*) Your answer is wather ambiguous. (*Slight pause*) And so this is Washington.

GEORGIE. That is not what you were saying.

SIR C. Perhaps not, but it will do. The last time I was in this countwy I was acquainted with a family in Washington—the Lovillons.

GEORGIE. You know the Lovillons? Why so do I. What a pretty girl Marie Lovillon is!

SIR C. (*Drily.*) Oh, yes.

GEORGIE. You say that as if it were anything but your opinion. Don't you like her?

SIR C. Not extwavagantly.

GEORGIE. (*Quickly.*) Why?

SIR C. She's not my style exactly. Were she more like you, for instance, I should pwobably like her bettah.

GEORGIE. (*Coldly.*) I value your compliment at its true worth. Were she in my place, no doubt you would have said the same thing.

SIR C. (*Calmly.*) It is possible.

GEORGIE. (*Scornfully.*) Your effrontery is admirable.

SIR C. And my temper imperturbable.

GEORGIE. And your impudence magnificent.

SIR C. And my admiwation bestowed where I think pwoper.

GEORGIE. You're no gentleman.

SIR C. But a peer of the realm, and a lord of the manor.

GEORGIE. Your birth or your queen may make you a lord, but not a gentleman.

SIR C. Come, now, why should you grow angwy at my humble little attempt to say in an indiwect way that I—like you?

GEORGIE. I am duly grateful.

SIR C. And that evah since I came to your father's house I have been—I have been——

GEORGIE. (*More graciously.*) You have been what?

SIR C. Let me see, how long have I been here?

GEORGIE. About a week. But you were saying that you have been something during that time.

SIR C. Yes, yes. I have been—I think I have been getting foolish, as I said before. Ah, well! When it is happiness to be foolish (*looks fondly at her*), 'tis foolishness not to be happy.

GEORGIE. (*Very graciously.*) Sir Charles, you seem to *feel* love, while other people only talk it.

SIR C. Did I speak of love?

GEORGIE. I thought so.

SIR C. Then it must be because you are my auditor. Generally I wegard love as a disease, the distinguishing chawacteristic of which is a tendency to convey the most commonplace ideas in ultra-human language. With you for a listener, howevah, it would seem almost appwopwiate.

GEORGIE. Indeed! What would seem almost appropriate?

SIR C. To expwess a man's feeling for you in any combination of hyperbolical words such as lovers use.

GEORGIE. I wonder if I have anything to do with the feelings which prompt you to talk thus.

SIR C. By heaven, you have.

GEORGIE. How am I to know it?

SIR C. Do not laugh, and I'll play at love like the veriest lover of them all.

GEORGIE. Like you have played at it in New York, for instance.

SIR C. Egad! but this is too much. You mock me. You seem to have a hidden meaning in your words. What mean you?

GEORGIE. Oh, nothing. Only uncle incidentally mentioned one day that he thought you and Mr. Tom Blassy were sighing to get back to New York, especially as he had promised to introduce you to two lady professionals whom you had seen giving an exhibition of their talent.

SIR C. Miss Wosewell, you know that your uncle is a most

abominable joker, **always twifling with other people's most**
tender feelings. (*Aside.*) A villain! A base villain!

GEORGIE. Sir Charles, I will believe you, and take your
word for it that you are only now *playing* at love.

SIR C. Egad! I have a mighty leaning to it.

GEORGIE. Some day you'll play at it in earnest, and *be* "the
veriest lover of them all," or I'm no prophetess.

SIR C. Methinks the day has come—the hour—and the
woman. Can you not see that evah since I have known you—
since that happy day when——

GEORGIE. (*Naively.*) When you said that all American
ladies (or *women*, if you would rather have it)—that a'l American women were affected; that they laughed too much; and
that the girls giggled immoderately at the most commonplace
remarks.

SIR C. Ah, then you have not forgotten that little scene on
shipboard. I have been in your thoughts sometimes, it seems.

GEORGIE. Yes, I have occasionally thought about you.

SIR C. And I—I have *always* thought about *you*.

GEORGIE. Always?

SIR C. Always

GEORGIE. And nothing more than *thought* about me?

SIR C. Yes, from the first you have been my idol. Your
image has evah been in my heart, and I have fallen down before it, worshiping it always. (*Clasps her waist.*) Will you
permit me to continue worshiping?

GEORGIE. (*Archly.*) Well, I don't know. I think I had
better; for perhaps that is the only way to get my revenge for
the many disagreeable things you have said about the Americans, Sir Charles.

SIR C. (*With a sly look.*) The truth is always disagwee-
able, Miss Wose—I mean Georgie. (*Slight pause.*) And it
was nevah more so than when you told me that the English
were the most selfish, egotistical, and arwogant people on the
face of the earth; and that I was the most selfish, egotistical,
and arwogant of them all—because, you see, I think you were
half wight.

GEORGIE. Well, if I were half right, and you were half
right, let us make it wholly right. (*Holds up her lips for a kiss,
and Sir Charles kisses her unctiously.*) But I wonder if you will
always be willing to so candidly acknowledge your faults.

SIR C. Always, when my deah wife uses her persuasive
voice to convince me that I am wong.

GEORGIE. Ah, I'm afraid not, especially if I am using my

persuasive voice to convince you that it is wrong to go out of an evening and leave your wife at home. But there is one thing, Charley——

SIR C. (*Slightly disgusted.*) Not " Charley," my deah ; but " Charles," if you think "*Sir* Charles " too formal now.

GEORGIE. Well, there is one thing, Charles, I want you to acknowledge ; and that is, that we are not such a very peculiar people as you once said we were.

SIR C. I do acknowledge it from the bottom of my heart. Still I must say that, though you may not be such a vewy peculiar people, yet *you*, my deah, are a vewy peculiar person.

GEORGIE. I a peculiar person ? And why ?

SIR C. Why ? Because you are going to marwy *me*.

GEORGIE. (*Shyly*) Woman's ways are past finding out.

[*Exeunt, lovingly.*

Enter John Blassy, Mrs. Harpley, and Mrs. Duckerson, who take a retired seat that is barely able to hold the three.

BLASSY. Here I flatter meself we shall not be observed. Take a seat, ladies.

MRS H. No prying eyes to see what we are doing. (*Sits down in one corner of the seat.*

MRS. D. And no rascally husband to note the peculiarities of the situation. (*Sits down in the other corner.*)

BLASSY. (*Squeezing himself in between the two ladies.*) Ha! ha! ha! " Peculiarities of the situation " is good. A jelly-fish between two sardines could not be more peculiar. I feel like a jelly-fish.

MRS. D. Which means that we are two sardines.

BLASSY No, no, no! You put a wrong construction on my words. I said——

MRS. D. Did you not understand it so, Alice ?

MRS. H. Not exactly. Even if it were possible to construe it so, Mr. Blassy did not mean it so He is too good-natured.

BLASSY. (*Patting her under the chin.*) That's a good little dear. It ought to be kissed, so it ought.

MRS. D. Am I in the way, Alice ?

MRS. H. Not at all, Nellie; not at all. (*In an undertone.*) Is she, Mr. Blassy ?

BLASSY. No, no, no—certainly not. (*Aside*) Though one thorn in me side would be enough.

MRS. D. I think we shall have a double wedding soon.

BLASSY. (*Startled.*) A double wedding! What, in the

Mormon style—two women marry one man? Ladies, you do not mean me.

MRS. H. (*Both ladies laughing.*) Why no, Mr. Blassy; we haven't proposed to you yet. The double wedding Nellie refers to is that of your son Tom to Clara, and Sir Charles to Georgie. They have been so inseparable of late that it has become the talk of the household.

BLASSY. Tom—my son—going to marry? Going to marry so soon? Well, well! how could it be otherwise? I knew it must come some day. And I shall be left alone in my old age. (*He hangs his head pathetically.*)

MRS. H. Do not take it so to heart, Mr. Blassy. There are always good friends in the world.

BLASSY. But none to cheer me.

MRS. H. Yes, some to cheer you.

MRS. D. (*Slyly.*) And some even to love you.

BLASSY. You, Mrs. Duckerson, talking that way—you, a married woman. I—I—never——

MRS. D. Never thought that you were fascinating enough to inspire a woman with love; but you are

MRS. H. Nellie, *do* stop your nonsense. What with you and George, Mr. Blassy's life is a burden.

MRS. D. Yes, a burden greater than most men's.

MRS. H. And one, perhaps, that he does not propose to increase by marrying.

BLASSY. What—what in the name of common sense is all this about? What have I said to cause all this? Here I am bemoaning me son's marriage, and then thrown all at once into a discussion of me own. It must be another joke conceived by that villain—I mean your varry 'umorous husband, Mrs. Duckerson.

MRS. D. No, he is not in this plot. Only Alice and I.

MRS. H. Do, *do* stop your ridiculous nonsense. What does Mr. Blassy care what we think about him?

MRS. D. "We," indeed! "*We!*" I did not mean myself at all.

BLASSY. Bless your 'arts, ladies, I love you all. There's only three things worth living for, and——

MRS. H. And what are they, Mr. Blassy?

BLASSY. They are women, wit, and wine. You see, I alter the order in which some other poet has said the same thing.

MRS. D. (*Looking quizzically at his figure.*) Some other poet?

BLASSY. Yes. The other poet said: "Wit, wine, and

women." You observe that I place women first, because with them are associated all the domestic joys—and—and things of that sort. (*Both ladies nod affirmatively.*) Next I place wit, because with that is associated all the joys of mixing with men of sense—like myself. (*Both ladies smile affirmatively.*) Last I place wine, because, you see, that is more, I may say—more of an animal joy; but still—a *great* joy. (*Aside, unctiously.*) And perhaps, after all, the *greatest* joy, without which the other two would at times be very tame.

MRS. H. (*All three rising from their seats.*) Mr. Blassy, you seem to be something of a philosopher as well as a poet. I could sit at your feet and drink wisdom for hours.

MRS. D. Then sit, Alice, sit; don't get up yet. I must be going. I suppose George will be looking all over for me.

MRS. H. Nonsense. He knows you are in good company. But go—go if you want to. We'll not detain you. I guess Mr. Blassy and I can interest each other, can't we Mr. Blassy?

BLASSY. Why, bless my 'art, yes. Of course, of course. But that is no reason why we——

Enter Georgie and Clara hurriedly

GEORGIE. Why, here they are. Where have you been? We have been looking for you all over.

CLARA. We want you to come into the kitchen to-night. We are going to have a dance?

MRS. D. A dance, indeed! What kind of a dance?

GEORGIE. A real plantation breakdown. Will you all come?

MRS. H. Of course we will come. I suppose you dance, Mr. Blassy?

BLASSY. Bless your little souls, ladies, my dancing days are a thing of the past.

MRS. D. Humbug. You are as full of the agility of youth as an alderman's pocket is of boodle.

GEORGIE. Why certainly he is. Here, aunties, get hold, and let us make a Tucker of him, and show him how easy it is.

The four ladies join hands, dance around Blassy a few times, and then all give him a good push.

BLASSY. Ha! ha! ha! That is immense. H'm It brings back the callow days of me youth. I shall be there.

CLARA. That will be just too lovely.

GEORGIE. Yes, and old Jake says he will play the violin and call the figures.

CLARA.   And we have asked Kate to bring her beau and a few friends.

GEORGIE.   To make it look like the real thing, you know, Mr. Blassy.

BLASSY.   How nice

MRS. H.   We shall be there.

MRS. D.   All in good time, and we shall certainly bring Mr. Blassy along.

BLASSY.   Who will most willingly consent to be brought by such fair creatures.

CLARA.   Don't forget.

GEORGIE.   If you do, we know where to look for you now.

MRS. H.   We shall not forget.

[Exeunt Georgie and Clara.

MRS. H.   (*Continuing.*)   And so you will have to dance now, Mr. Blassy.

MRS. D.   Of course he will; and I shall claim him for my partner.

MRS. H   I was going to claim that honor for myself.   Now, which do you prefer, Mr. Blassy?

MRS. D.   Yes, which do you prefer?

They both look lovingly up to his face.

BLASSY.   (*Looking first at one and then the other.*)   How happy ought I be, indeed!   The right and left bower in my hand.

BOTH.   But which is the right bower?

BLASSY.   H'm.   I never thought o' that.   I can hardly tell the right bower from the left.   I'm only new to the game.   So you will have to settle it between yourselves, me dears.   I'm the little joker.   (*Offers his arms, and they move off.*)   For meself, I never knew before that I was such a great ladies' man.   But 'tis a queer world, and we know not—we know not——

[Exeunt.

SCENE 2.—*Kitchen in Mr. Rosewell's house, cleared of everything except a bench, on which Jake is discovered tuning his violin. Enter Kate and her beau, and another colored couple, followed in a few seconds by Sir Charles, Tom, and Mr. Duckerson.   Then come Georgie and Clara, immediately followed by Blassy, Mrs. Duckerson, and Mrs. Harpley, the two ladies striving to outdo each other in fascination*

BLASSY.   Well, ladies, have you settled between yourselves your little difficulty?

DUCK. (*Getting hold of his wife's arm.*) Nellie, I want you for my partner.

MRS. D. You miserable wretch! I wanted to dance with Mr Blassy.

DUCK. Can't do it. Don't you see that Alice wants that —that distinguished honor herself?

MRS. D. I know it; and that is why I wanted to tantalize her.

DUCK. Perfectly womanlike. But then you might leave her a free field for once. And if you want to do any tantalizing, tantalize me; that's a little deary. Besides, old Bag-o'-Bones might tread on your toes, and then——

MRS. D. You're simply horrid. But we'll dance in their set, anyhow.

DUCK All right, but look out for your toes.

GEORGIE. Now, Jake, are you ready?

JAKE. Yes'm; yes'm.

GEORGIE. Then choose your partners.

Sir Charles, Georgie, Tom, and Clara occupy the right of the stage in front. Blassy, Mrs. Harpley, Mr. Ducker-son, and Mrs. Duckerson take up a position on the left in front Kate, her beau, and the other colored couple occupy the back of the stage. Jake starts up the music, the orchestra accompanying him; and he sings as follows, the rest also singing, but not so as to drown Jake's voice:

Choose yo' pardners; time's er-flying;
    Take yo' places on de flo'.
Don't yo' hear dat fiddle cryin'
    "Nickerdemus Ebbermo!"
S'lute yo' pardners! Bow perlitely.
    Dat's de motion through en through.
Swing dem corners! Step up lightly.
    Hail, Columby! Hallaloo!
Fus' fo' forward! Keep 'er diggin'.
    Now you sasshay back agin.
Neber mind yo' ragged riggin',
    So's 't don't show de naked skin.
Lawdy! see dat old man Blassy,
    How he bow en scrape aroun';
Head seems like a looking-glassy,
    Shines so bright up on de crown.

Ladies change, en keep 'er scootin'.
   Cross right ober, now you swing.
Hold dem heads up highfalutin';
   Look permiskus, dat's de thing.
Mussy! look at Missy Georgie!
   Dat gal flings a supple toe.
Crack yo' heels dar, Massa Charlie;
   Bow en smile, en—" so en so."
Balance all! Now don't git lazy.
   Fly aroun' en tar yo' shirt.
Stomp dem feet, but don't go crazy,
   Else Mam Harpley sho' git hurt.
Fiddler got his mouf wide open'm,
   Holin' down de music tight;
Teeth, dey settin' sorter slop'm,
   Look like tomestones in de night.
All sasshay! I clar to gracious,
   Nebber seed de like befo';
White folks sho'ly dance audacious
   When dey hab an open flo'.
Heb'nly kingdom! look at Clary,
   Bofe eyes shining like de moon.
" Don't git w'ary, don't git w'ary,"
   Dat's de way to change de chune.
Promernade all! Now dat comes handy.
   Hunt yo' seats en take a res'.
Gentermens will pass de candy
   To de gal he love de bes'.

THE END.